Disney · PIXAR
FINDING DORY

A Fin-tastic Adventure

FINDDORY4243

Code is valid for your Finding Dory ebook and may be redeemed through the Disney Story Central app on the App Store. Content subject to availability. Parent permission required. Code expires on December 31, 2019.

Bath · New York · Cologne · Melbourne · Delhi
Hong Kong · Shenzhen · Singapore

Pick a Path

Dory is swimming to meet her friends Marlin and Nemo, but she's forgotten the way! Help her find her pals by tracing the right path through the maze.

Start

Finish

Good work!

Give yourself a sticker.

Answer on page 31

Hurry, Hank!

Hank and Dory are on the move. Only two of these pictures are exactly alike. Can you spot and circle them?

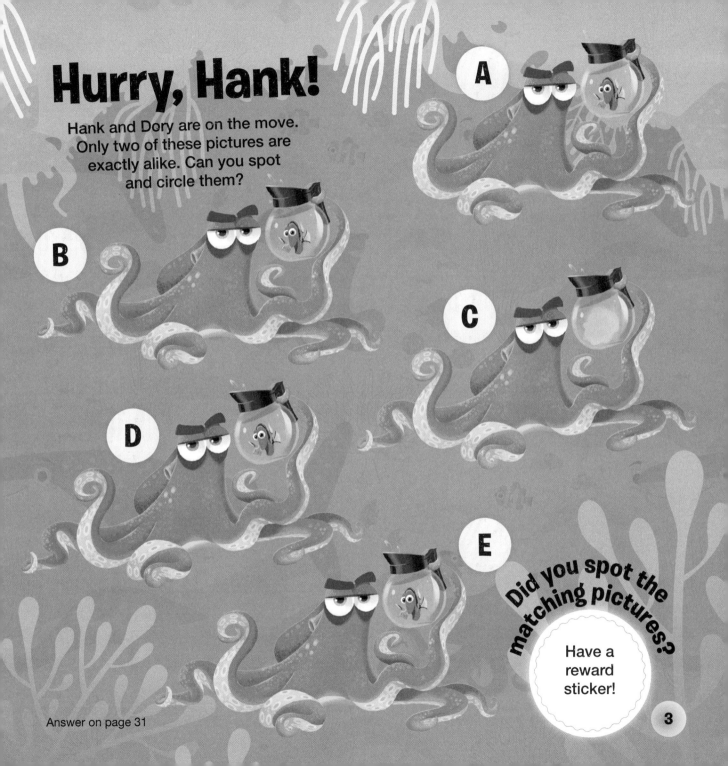

A

B

C

D

E

Did you spot the matching pictures?

Have a reward sticker!

Answer on page 31

Ocean Word Search

Dory is a very forgetful fish! To help her remember her name, find and circle DORY as many times as you can in the grid below. Look up, down, forward, and backward.

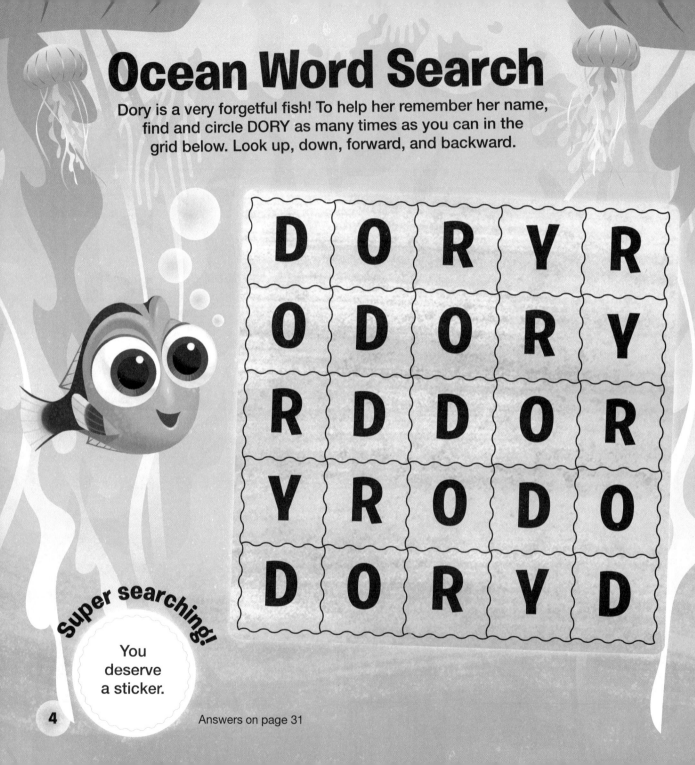

D	O	R	Y	R
O	D	O	R	Y
R	D	D	O	R
Y	R	O	D	O
D	O	R	Y	D

Answers on page 31

Sea Lion Shadows

Can you draw lines to link the three sea lions—
Fluke, Gerald, and Rudder—to their shadows?

All matched up!

Add your sticker.

Draw Dory

Using the grid as a guide, copy the picture of Dory, then add her bright blue tang colors.

Cool copying!

Give yourself a reward sticker.

Odd Pal Out

Nemo and his friends Tad and Sheldon are playing on the reef.
Can you spot and circle the odd picture out in each row?

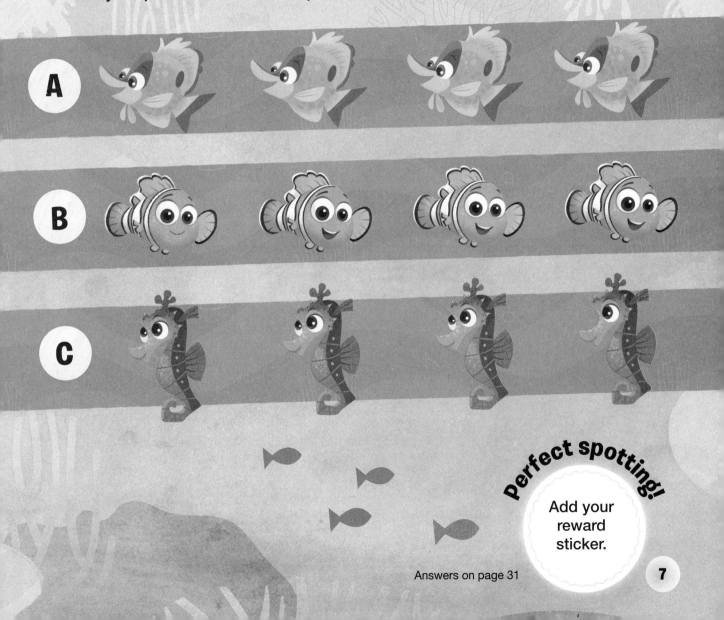

Answers on page 31

Careful, Dory!

Dory thinks jellyfish look cute and squishy! How many jellyfish can you count in the ocean?

Good counting!

Give yourself a sticker.

Answer on page 31

New Friends

Dory has made some fin-tastic new friends! Trace over the letters to spell out their names.

Hank

Destiny

Bailey

Now add your super reward sticker!

Place it here.

Hug Time!

Who is going to get cuddled by the friendly otter? Follow the lines to find out.

Hug-tastic!

Now place your sticker.

Answer on page 31

Septopus Sudoku

Hank has camouflage capabilities and can blend in anywhere. Make sure each camouflaged Hank appears only once in each row, column, and mini grid by correctly coloring the empty boxes.

Answers on page 31

You deserve a reward sticker!

Add it here.

Happy Family

Find and circle five differences between these two pictures of baby Dory and her parents, Charlie and Jenny.

Place
your
reward
sticker.

Answers on page 31

Seven-Legged Shadow

Hank has seven legs, so he's a septopus! Find and circle the shadow that exactly matches the picture of Hank.

A

B

C

D

Did you find it?

Add your reward sticker here!

Answer on page 31

Becky to the Rescue!

Becky the loon likes Marlin, and she wants to help him find Dory! Lead Becky through the maze to reach Marlin.

Start

Finish

You made it!

Give yourself a sticker.

Answer on page 31

Starfish Sums

Can you help Dory complete these sums?
Write your answers in the bubbles.

A ★ ★ + ★ ★ ★ = ◯

B ★ ★ ★ ★ - ★ = ◯

C ★ ★ ★ ★ ★ + ★ ★ ★ = ◯

Answers on page 31

Math superstar!

Reward yourself with a sticker.

Colorful Coral Reef

Dory, Nemo, and Marlin live in a coral reef with lots of other fish. Draw and color a deep-sea scene filled with coral, shells, and seaweed!

Reward Stickers

Just for Fun!

That looks awesome!

Now add a sticker.

17

Color Sequences

Dory is a blue and yellow fish. Can you help her complete these sequences by adding the missing color?

A

B

C

D

You got it!

Add your reward sticker.

Answers on page 31

Draw Destiny

Using the grid as a guide, copy the picture of Destiny, and then add her whale shark spots.

19

Happy Home

Marlin and Nemo live in an anemone.
Join the dots to complete their
home, then color it in.

Home sweet home!

Have a
reward
sticker.

Thanks, Hank!

Find and circle five differences between these two pictures of Dory and her helpful pal Hank.

Answers on page 32

Found all five?

Give yourself a sticker.

Splashing Sea Lions

Fluke, Gerald, and Rudder are swimming through the ocean. Can you trace along their trails with a pencil, without touching the sides?

Start

Start

Start

Top tracing!

Place your sticker.

Dory Speaks Whale.

Figure out what Dory's saying by copying every other letter from the bubbles into the boxes. The first one has been done for you!

Start

| J | | | |

Answer on page 32

Answer on page 32

You speak whale, too!

Add a sticker.

23

On the Reef

Can you match each piece from the panel to the correct place in the puzzle? Circle the piece that is not part of the puzzle.

Answers on page 32

24

Colorful Fish

The ocean is full of fin-tastic fish!
Give each fish below a tropical pattern,
and then add some bright colors.

Those fish look color-ific!

Have a
sticker.

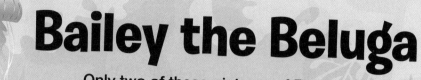

Bailey the Beluga

Only two of these pictures of Bailey are
exactly alike. Can you spot and circle them?

A

B

C

D

E

F

Answer on page 32

Did you spot the matching pictures?

Place your reward sticker.

26

Dreaming Dory

What is baby Dory dreaming about?
Draw it in the thought bubble below!

Great work!

Give yourself a sticker.

A Busy Ocean

How many fish can you count in each shoal?
Write the totals in the bubbles.

All added up!

Answers on page 32

Pretty Patterns

Starfish come in lots of different colors and patterns!
Trace over the patterns on the starfish below.

Super starfish!

Now add
a sticker.

29

A Family Again

Dory has remembered her mom and dad! Help her reach them by picking the correct path through the maze.

Start

Finish

Found the right route?

You deserve a sticker!

Answer on page 32

Answers

Page 2

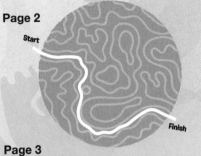

Page 3
B and E

Page 4
DORY appears 7 times

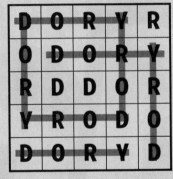

Page 5

Page 7

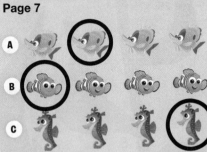

Page 8
8 jellyfish

Page 10
Destiny is going to get cuddled.

Page 11

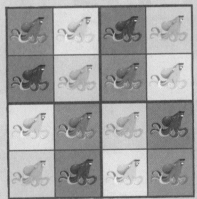

Page 12

Page 13
Shadow D

Page 14

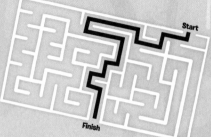

Page 15
A—5
B—3
C—7

Page 18

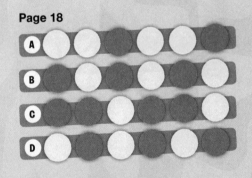

31

Answers

Page 21

Page 28

5

7

6

8

Page 23
Just keep swimming

Page 24

Page 30

Start

Finish

Page 26
B and F